INFINITY PUBLISHING

praise for Oliver Lewis & You're Not The Only One

"Very touching, extremely heartfelt,
beautifully written.
(An) emotional journey bringing (readers)
into the fold of four friends, left with a
warm glow."

-beta reader

"A rising star in the literary world"
"Oliver Lewis is reaching for the stars."

-InYourArea

OLIVER LEWIS

is the author of the *Manes Assassins series*,
he has been praised as "an up and
coming young author"
You can usually find him at his desk
writing stories or reading the day away.
His other favourite things include his
friends, indie music and coffee. He
currently resides in Wales with his family.

You're Not The Only One
a verse novella
Oliver Lewis

INFINITY PUBLISHING

Infinity Publishing

First Edition: 20th August 2021

Copyright © 2021, Oliver Lewis

All rights reserved. This book or any portion thereof
may not be reproduced or used in any manner whatsoever
without the express written permission of the publisher
except for the use of brief quotations in a book review.

L.SRC, Milton Keynes, UK

Cover image & graphics: Shutterstock & Sparklestroke

Cover design: Oliver Lewis

<u>**All photographs featured on grey pages taken by Oliver Lewis**</u>

**Please be aware that this book contains sensitive content
(implicitly or explicitly) relating to:
homophobia, bullying, strong language**

MORE BY OLIVER LEWIS AND AVAILABLE FROM INFINITY PUBLISHING

young adult fiction

BLOODCROSS
YOU'RE NOT THE ONLY ONE

for older readers

THE HANDPICKED DEATH OF A VOICE AT DUSK (MANES ASSASSINS #1)
THE REVIVAL OF A PECULIAR KIND - PART ONE (MANES ASSASSINS #2)

YOU'RE NOT THE ONLY ONE

a verse novella

OLIVER LEWIS

Wallow in the mire and then you're at the pinnacle
The fabricated smiles so wide, that it hurts
Your composure is so brittle, and you hold yourself so well
Inside, you cling to pieces of a broken carousel
Tonight these streets are heaving
With young hearts on the chase

-Sam Fender, You're Not the Only One

for the hopeful ones.

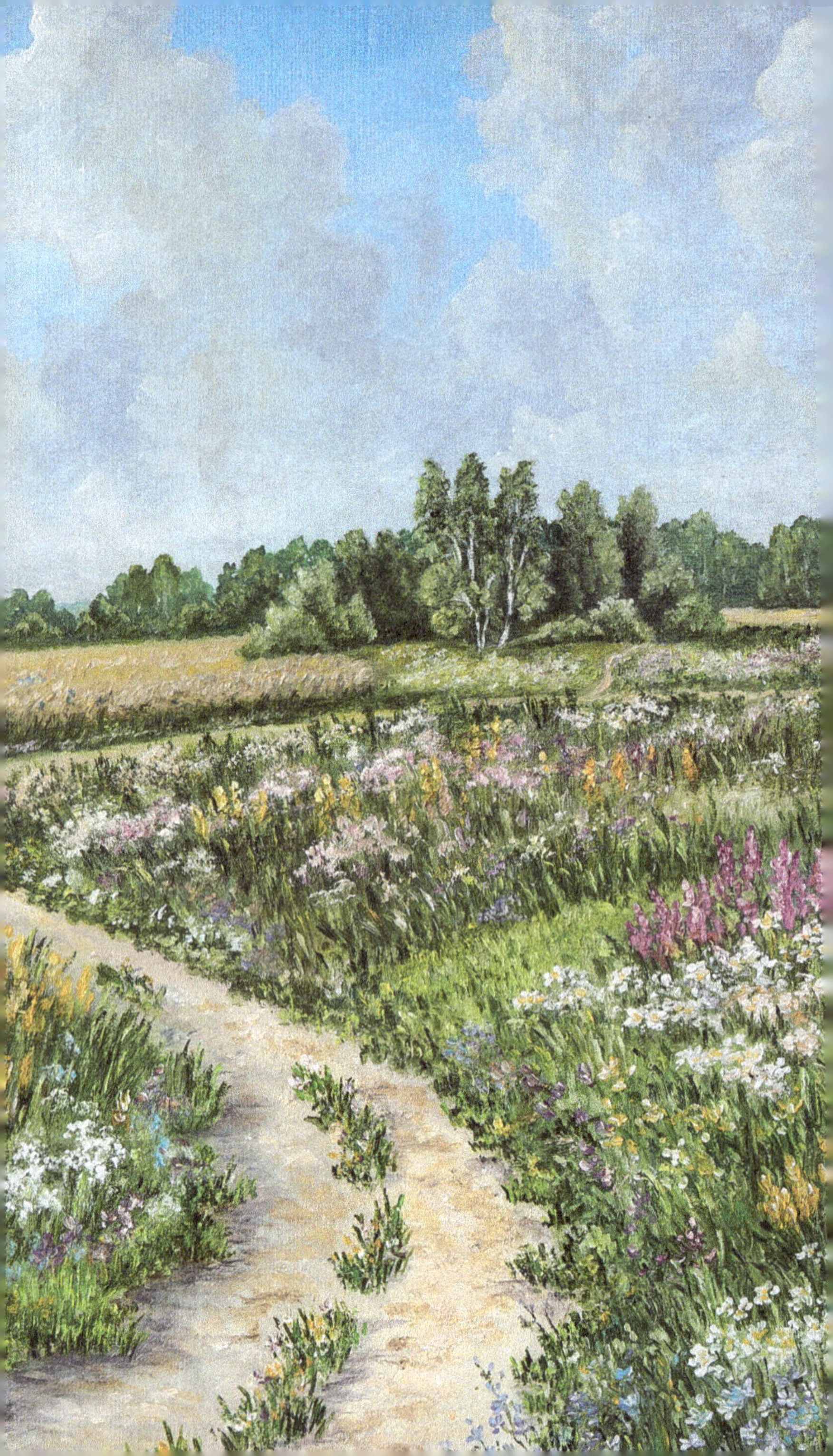

CHAPTER ONE
SUMMER

*If you're reading this,
I'm glad, but also,
I'm nervous.
And that's okay,
we're all nervous sometimes.*

*If you feel like, when you reach the end—if you reach the end,
that this book was written for you,
it was.*

*If you live through this narrator for the next few hours,
days,
weeks,
be honest with yourself,
if only for a mere moment.*

*If you are high on the possibilities of the dark,
just know that one day,
you'll be high on the possibilities of the light, too.*

*If all, or even some of these words you seem to be part of;
these words of raw and true feeling,
of angst, joy, uncertainty, and pride,
I hope that you have a small epiphany...
that you're not the only one.*

YOU'RE NOT THE ONLY ONE

Sometimes I

wonder
why,
I am not like them.

OLIVER LEWIS

The birds are alive and kicking,
singing their hearts out.

You could even hear them over the traffic.

I'm leaving school pleased with myself,
I got the grades that I wanted – needed,
and I walk away from that building without looking back.

I'll probably never set foot in there again.

Starting sixth form next year, I am.
The same place as my friends.

Hopefully the people there won't be as bad as they were where I've just left.
Not all of them were b a d of course.
In-fact, ninety five percent of them were completely good.

> *But five percent can be a lot when*
> *you feel like you're*
> *on your own.*

I'm pacing frantically, feeling a flurry of emotions as I do so.
I decide to take the long way home,
so that I don't come across the ones who call me
queer
as an insult.

YOU'RE NOT THE ONLY ONE

Isn't it scary to know that people can use your
truth
as an insult?

But seems they're not here,
I can focus all my energy on being excited for tonight.

In just a few hours, I'll be with my friends,
singing my heart out to songs that mean the
everything to me.
Singing my heart out to songs that have gotten me
through the roughest of times,
and the happiest of times.

I smile,
I embrace the sunshine,

I breathe in the
sweet
summer
air.

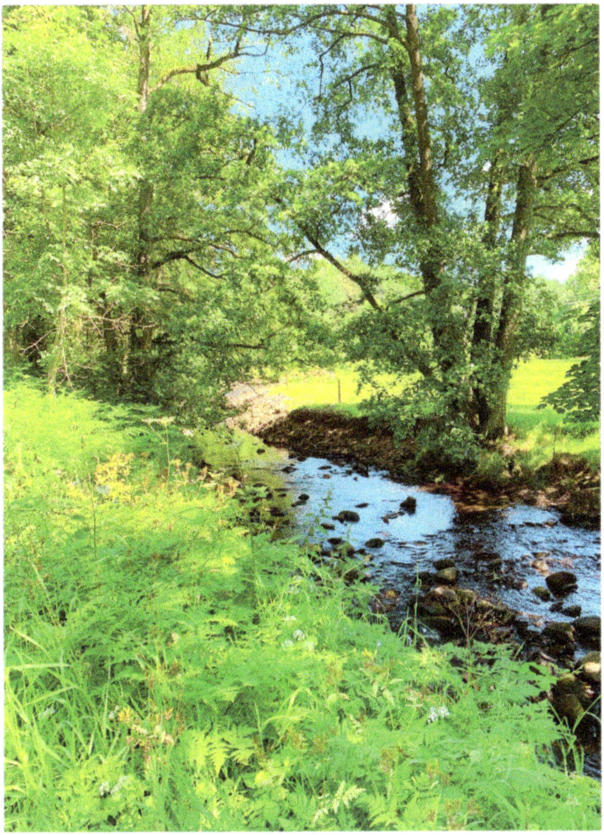

I read lots of books.
I hear people talk about how important a
D I V E R S E
cast is, and I shrugged it off as I do with most things.
But now I realise how very, very important it is.
Because diversity is all around us and we are all part
of it, the bubble of diversity, in our own little ways.

And I guess I've found where I fit in.

When I arrive home,
I am greeted by the cheerful guitar riffs for my indie playlist.
My three best friends
Archie
Elijah
and George
are sitting in the living room.

I can faintly hear my Mum pottering in the kitchen,
but hardly.

"Leo!"
Elijah greets me, the other two smile.
Slouched on the sofa,
still in their college attire.
Suit, tie.
Very smart indeed.

I grin and fall back onto the sofa between them,
dropping my backpack to the floor.

"That's it. You're done." George says.
With school, with GCSEs, he means.
Nodding, I reply "Yup!"
I can't help the corners of my lips curling up slightly,
a faint smile surfacing.
I chuckle, shake my head a little.
"I'm *done!*"
Archie laughs.

I head up to my room to get changed for the concert,
I don't know what to wear.

I stare at my wardrobe, trying not to dwell on the matter,
but I can't help staring at my clothes and notice how
m u n d a n e
they seem.

If only I could muster up some confidence,
act how I want to act,
wear what I want to wear,
appear, look however I want.

But if there's anyone I can do that around, it's them boys downstairs,
if there's one night I should be doing this,
it's
tonight.

Alas, I dress in black jeans and a mustard yellow jumper,
might as-well wear my favourite colour at least.
I sigh, stare out of the window for a moment,
and roll up my jeans a little.

"Leo?"
I hear George outside the door.
"You ready?"
"Yeah." I reply.
And then he asks me one of the hardest questions

ever for me to answer,
so causally, like it's nothing,
and of course, to normal people it *is* nothing. But to me...

"How you feeling?"

OLIVER LEWIS

HOW

YOU'RE NOT THE ONLY ONE

YOU

OLIVER LEWIS

FEELING

YOU'RE NOT THE ONLY ONE

?

Despite the weight of the question:
'how are you feeling?'
we always tend to reply with something like:
I'm good
I'm fine
fine
fine?

What does
fine
even mean?

It hardly sounds like you're firing on
all cylinders, does it?

Maybe sometimes it's worth being honest with ourselves,
but not today.

YOU'RE NOT THE ONLY ONE

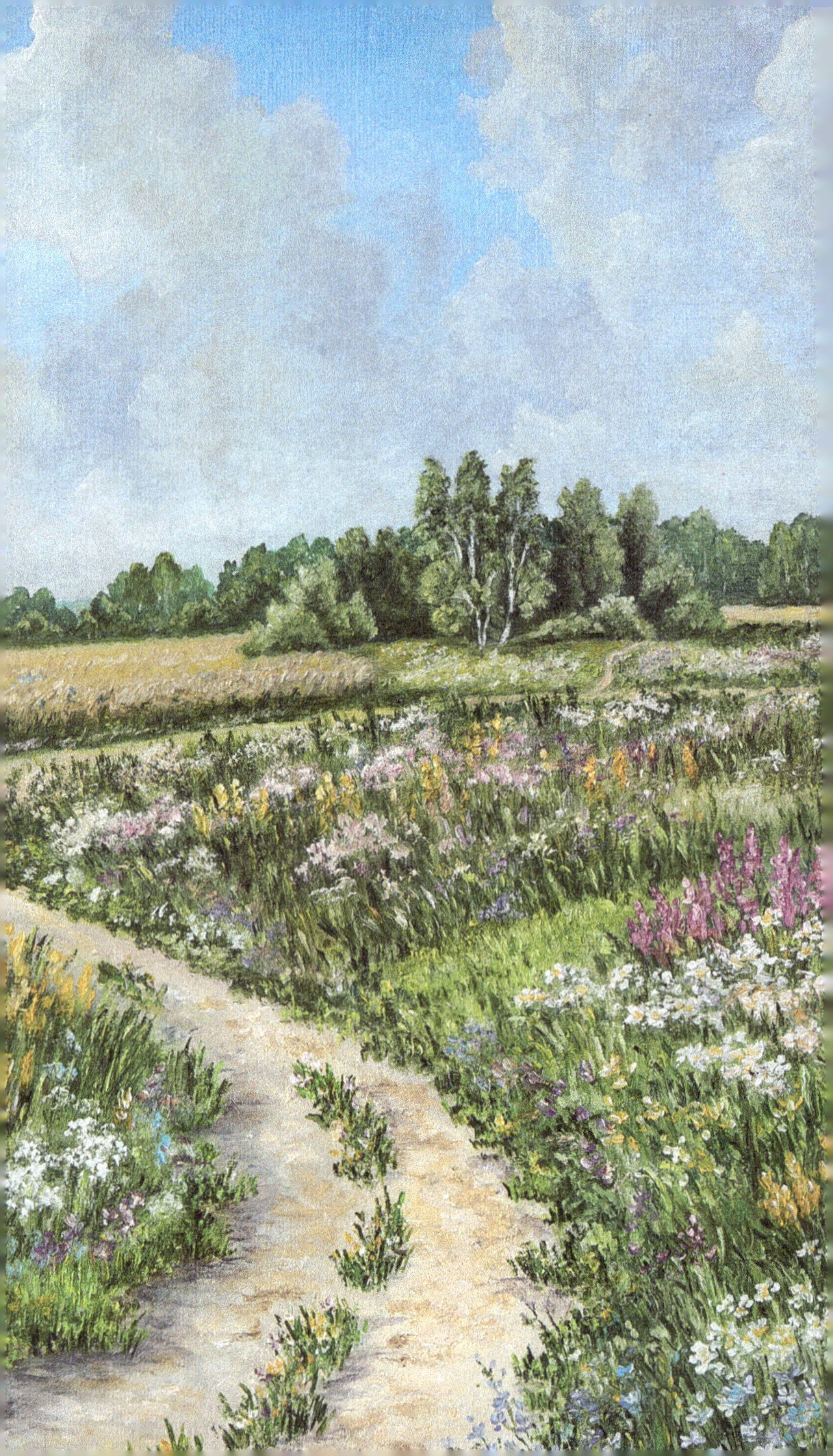

CHAPTER TWO
MUSIC

We need to leave in an hour,
so whilst we wait,
drinks are opened and conversations are had.

"I bet you're excited for A-Levels, eh?" Elijah nudges me,
and I smile, because he's smiling,
and seeing my friends smile makes *me* smile.

"Honestly, you don't even understand!" I reply,
and it's true.
I don't think anyone understands how excited I am to
say *au revoir* to sciences, and maths.
All I've ever wanted to do is create,
tell stories,
learn how stories are told,
take deep dives into *how* stories are told.

And I know you think I'm crazy,
and that's fine.

YOU'RE NOT THE ONLY ONE

We walk to the train station from my house.
On the stroll, we all discuss Italy,
reminding each other to be round mine early on Monday morning,
not to forget passports,
and to pack whatever the fuck we want to wear,
because the only people seeing us,
is us.
Not that that should make a difference, but sadly,
it does.

> *Because it's a summer night,*
> *the sun is just beginning to set.*
> *Up above is a beautiful ombre of orange,*
> *with red streaks through remaining clouds,*
> *like veins of lava seeping through the sky.*

The train station is in sight now,
it's floodlights at the entrance piercing through the dusk,
and I'm sad, because the lights are ruining Mother Nature's dramatic display,
but also pleased and giddy as they beckon me closer to the platform,
closer to the concert.
Closer.

Our carriage is

empty

and

 quiet

YOU'RE NOT THE ONLY ONE

A few weeks ago,
I read a book.

When I finish the book,
I'm crying,

It was about these *two boys*,
meeting and
finding their place in the world.
It just caught me off-guard,
spoke to me,
to *me*?

How words can
make you feel feelings you've never felt before.

I've never felt this before.

Lost
but also like I've
found
something,
deep inside of me that was always there,
just waiting for the right moment
T o   S u r f a c e .

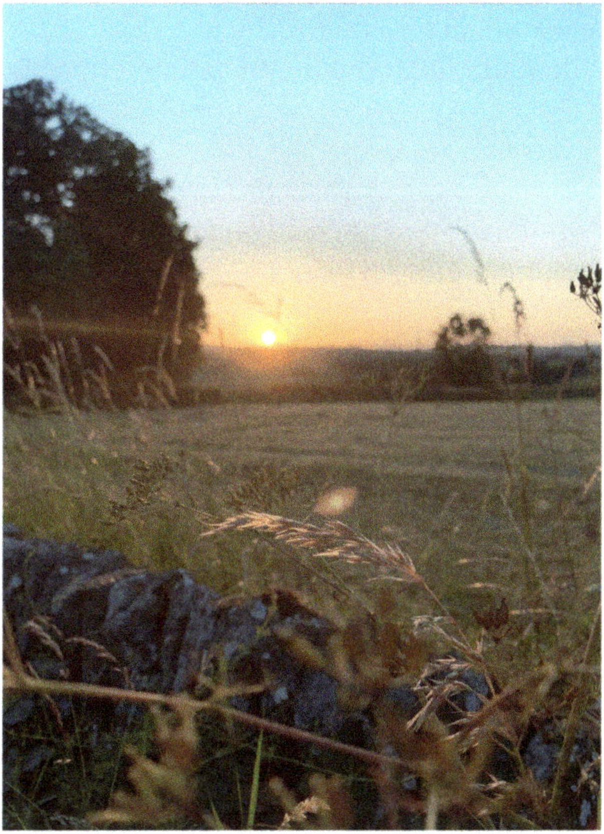

another few weeks ago...

It was so hot that day,
yet the grass still a little damp.
It was early on, maybe that's why,
a bit of dew still lingering on the pointed tips of the grass;
the sun was up.

We sat on the ground, picnic blanket below us,
books scattered around us.
There were classics
(battered spines an'all, yellowed pages, creased front covers)
There were new releases, some of our favourites,
some one of us liked and the other didn't.

Elijah's speaker blasted out songs requested by each of us,
good songs.

And yet,
"Song's crap!" Archie blurted, I scoff cause it kinda is.
George, who's choice it was punches Archie in the arm and he retaliates.
Archie jumps up and George follows, chasing after him.
I and Elijah chuckle at their childishness as they leg it across the field we're in.
They tackle each other to the ground,
and again, we laugh because they are like two little

kids.
As is everyone at heart.

*'And they could call it the great,
the great escape of the world.'
— The Lathums.*

OLIVER LEWIS

There's something calming about
hustle and bustle,
which sounds strange.

And yes, this is a strange thought,
but there's something calming,
quiet,
comforting,
about blending in.

In a busy city centre,
you blend in like you're invisible,
eavesdropping on various people's conversations,
just snippets,
as they pass you by, barely acknowledging your existence.

You may find this a bad thing,
the fact that someone could *be* so rude as to barely acknowledge your existence,
but I think otherwise.

You are in your own world,
in your own head,
with only the beings you care to be there with.

You may go about your business,
careless of the judgement of those around you.

As long as you can blend in,
you can be yourself

YOU'RE NOT THE ONLY ONE

to an extent...

That extent is society's expectations of us.

The societal expectations that fester like maggots in flesh with
privilege,
of being *white,*
of being *straight,*
of being *unrepressed.*

So maybe, we'll never be able to fully
express ourselves,
be ourselves,
until this damn society of ours bucks it's ideas up!

That's all to say we're in the city centre,
making our way to the venue.

The rumbling bass of the first support act thrums
through me as I stand at the bar.
I ask for a lemonade,
which Elijah will of course want to mix with the
Vodka in his hip flask,
I may kindly decline.

Merchandise is pinned tediously to a board,
t-shirts stretched out to the point where they could
quite possibly tear.
The least appealing way to display a t-shirt,
but I still want to buy one.

The concrete floor is sticky with condensation and
spilled alcohol,
shoes squeaking as we walk towards the 'standing'
entrance,
the bass getting stronger, until the doors are flung
open by a security guard, our tickets are scanned,
and the music envelops us.

YOU'RE NOT THE ONLY ONE

It's quite difficult to explain the feeling you get when you're at a concert,
so surreal it is almost as if you're not *actually there.*

Alas, the support acts had passed, and the venue filled to the brim with people.
We were all packed in like sardines, but in a *nice* way, which probably makes no sense.

Loud, muffled chatter surrounds us,
so much so, I have to shout so that Archie can hear me.
"You ready?"
"I'm *so ready*." He replies, and throws his arm around me.

And almost as if on cue,

the lights dim and plunge us into darkness.
Blue spotlights create a faint, dim glow from behind the stage,
allowing us to see the half-silhouettes of the band as they edge closer to filling this concert-hall with the most beautiful noise.

OLIVER LEWIS

The sound of *'You're Not The Only One'* fills the hall,
I could cry, I *do* cry, and I don't care.

When I blink, I keep my eyes shut for just a second longer than usual,
taking a moment to be in my own head,
but also not wanting to miss a second of what was going on around me.

George knows what this song means to me, so he subtly looks,
a small but sure smile spreads across his face.
I look back for a second, just a small, minuscule second,
and he looks at me like there's something worth looking at.
There's a light in his eyes, and he is to me and I am to him, briefly gorgeous.
A sensitive moment,
one for the time capsule,
one to treasure.

The music is too loud,
and yet,
it is not loud enough.

YOU'RE NOT THE ONLY ONE

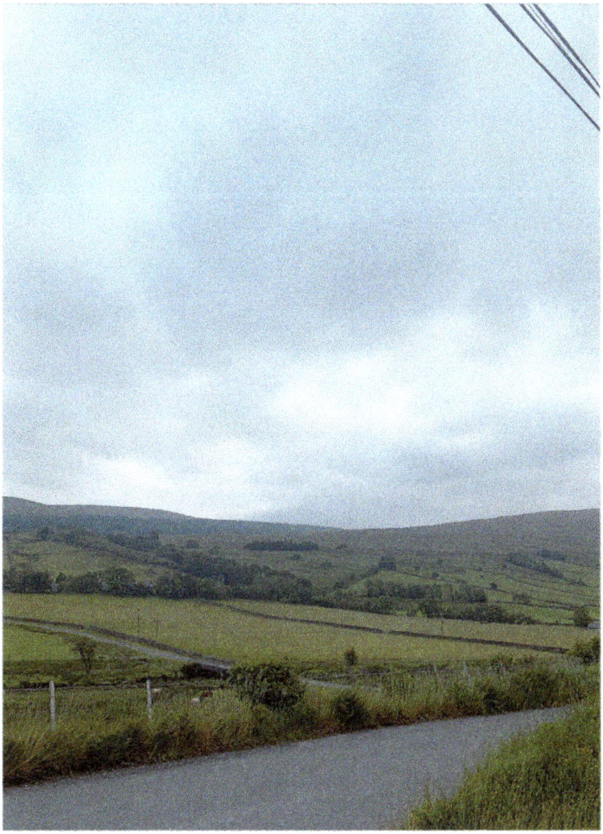

Being at an airport at 4am is
serene.

It is quiet, the occasional clack of footsteps echoing in the foyer.

Your eyes are hardly open.

You are happy, yet simply want not to be here.

How strange.

How **serene**.

YOU'RE NOT THE ONLY ONE

We're on the cheapest flight to Italy we could possibly find,
but it's surprisingly exhilarating.
For such a small cost,
you are about to travel such great distance.
Thus is true in life,
occasionally.

Three of us are squashed together on a row,
and Elijah sits across the aisle from us looking
slightly creeped out by the wrinkly old white guy next to him.
The man's gilet (seemingly as old as him) brushes Elijah's shoulder,
he looks across at us with a face of disgust, and as a reaction to his expression, Archie is silently creasing in the corner.
It's too difficult to hold it in, so I end up bursting out laughing as well,
the man gives me a *what the fuck?* kinda side-eye.

The plane hums loudly,
as if it were a living, breathing being.

But it's simply a machine,
simply a machine.

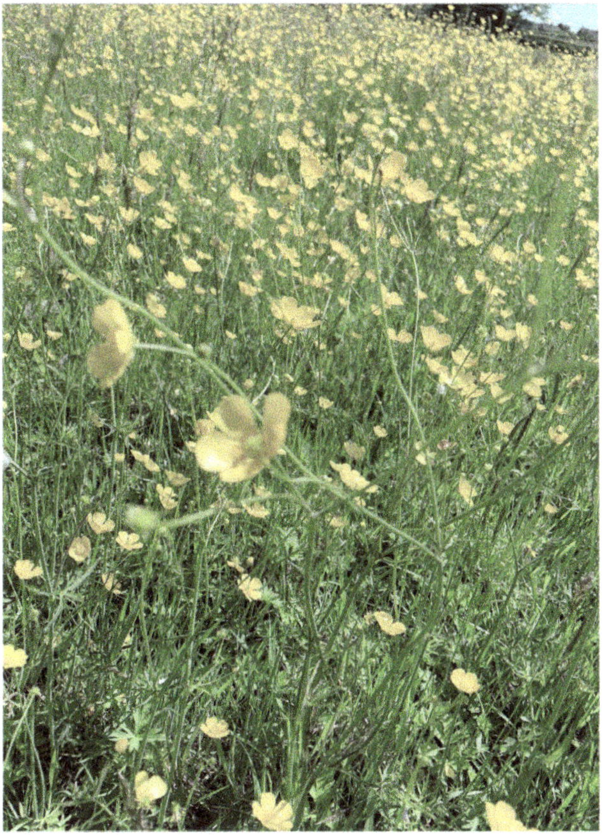

"I can't believe we paid additional fees for a suitcase full of books and vinyls!" George said.
Archie chuckled. "Imagine if they lost it."
"Don't *even!*" I joked.

YOU'RE NOT THE ONLY ONE

Upon the plane's landing, there was a cheer.
Was that a 'thank you Pilot' cheer?
Or was it a 'thank god we're still alive' cheer?
Because that plane was all over the place, and I'm surprised we're still here.

A wall of heat hits us as we exit the plane,
into the *Italy* heat.

The air is dry, but it is sweet.
It is sweet with the taste of freedom, and of four weeks reading,
exploring,
getting lost in music,
of sunsets,
of laughter with friends.

The air is dry, but it is sweet.
The sickly-sweet taste of freedom.

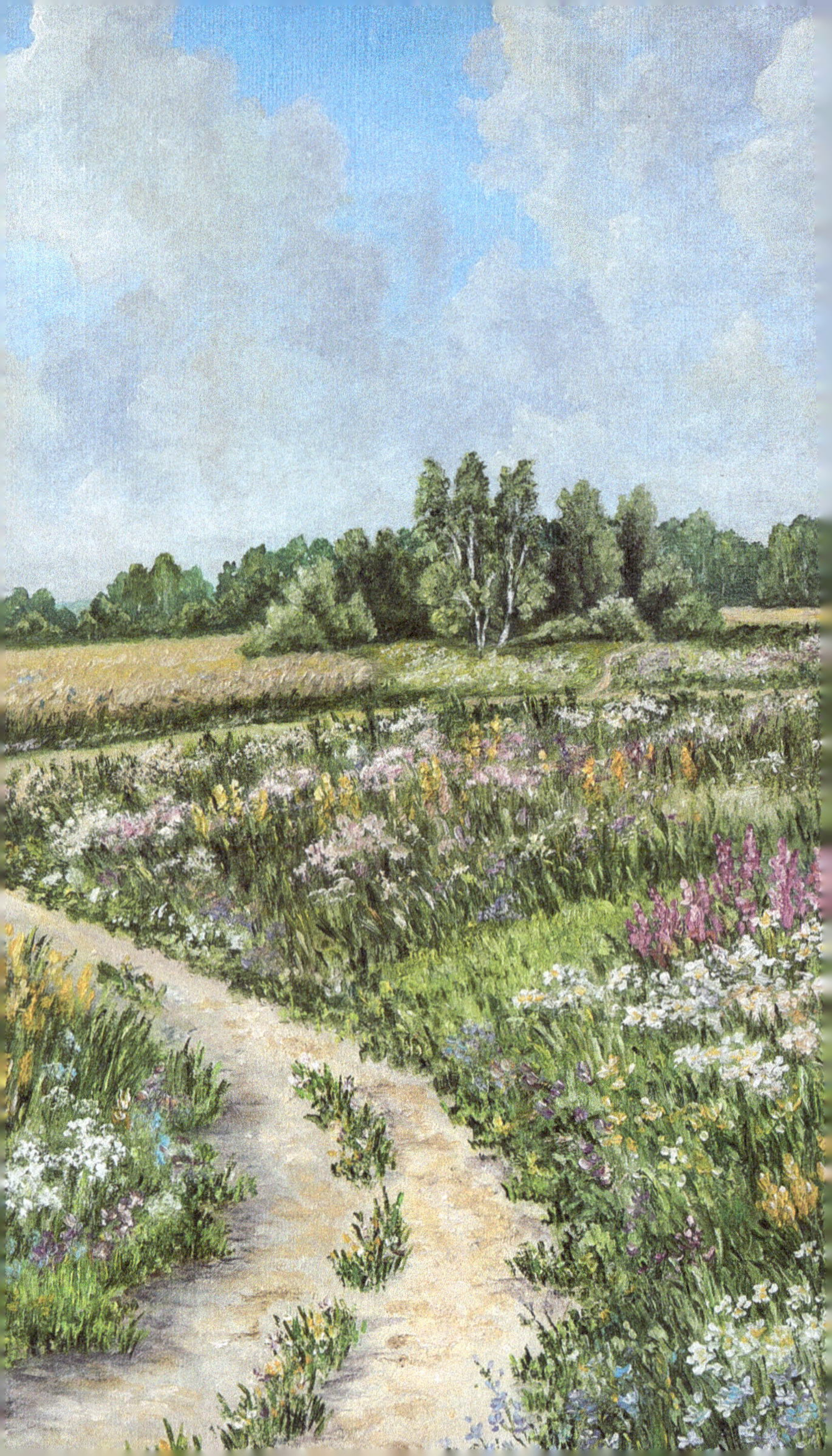

CHAPTER THREE
ITALY

The hotel was cheap,
but it's good enough for us.

Elijah throws his suitcase onto the duvet,
before collapsing backwards onto the bed.

I pull out a battered paperback of
The Invisible Life of Addie LaRue,
you can read your favourite book over and over,
it'll never get old.

There's me and him in a room,
George and Archie next door.

And after all the noise of travelling,
and airports,
and buses,
it is, for now,
quiet.

YOU'RE NOT THE ONLY ONE

Dawn breaks,
symbolising new beginnings.

It's like we are being welcomed into Italy by the Sun.

The Sun is
an invitation to start the day,
and venture into the maze of cobbles.

I crack open the window next to my bed,
looking out over the (usually busy) street below,
but there is not a soul **in sight** – an **insight** into the town,
before the early risers,
amble the alleyways.

The Sun is at work way before anyone else,
up there, warming the waters:
lakes, ponds, brooks and the sea,
cerulean as it is.

The Sun is at work way before anyone else,
up there, giving plants the affection they need,
to grow.

Giving light,
and giving life.

Elijah is surfacing from sleep now,
so I take that as my cue to get some coffee on.

The kettle in our room is small, but does the job,
it lets out a low hiss, a hum, slowly whirring to life.

It is loud, like everything.
Everything seems louder in the mornings.

Elijah is surfacing from sleep now,
so I take that as my cue to pour him a cup of coffee,
because I'm nice like that.

YOU'RE NOT THE ONLY ONE

I check my Instagram feed and find nothing new.

The latest photo is one from my old school,
it's of the football team.

Being simply curious, I take a look at the rest of the profile,
and there's the boys football team again,
and the boys rugby team,
and the boys basketball team
and...

My old school seemed to pride itself on sports,
which is fine, I suppose.

Continuing to scroll,
I long to find something other than a picture of a sports team,
or a trash one some teacher has took from the back of the hall during assembly.

You post things you're proud of, right?
Things that –in this case—would promote the school?

Are they not proud of the artists?
Are they not proud of the *girls* football team?

Are they not proud of that one boy in year 10 who joined the netball team,
and stuck up the middle finger to every other boy in year 10 who called him a 'big fucking girls blouse'?

That was two years back,
and I remember seeing this kid strut out of the
training session with the biggest grin I've ever seen,
and I remember sitting and talking to him that lunch
time.

And I remember being envious of his confidence.

I know deep down that if that kid was in my position,
(which he could've been for all I knew)
and *they* threatened to punch his head in,
or push his bike off the pavement on the way to
school,
or so much as muttered the 'g' of 'gay' as an insult,
he'd have turned round and
knocked
their
lights
out.

I should've done that too, really.

But still, my old school's Instagram page consists of
nothing but pictures of the *boys sports teams*,
where a few of the players were outright
homophobes.

My diary from the time read:

I love playing sports, but there's no way,
I'd play a match with some of them.

YOU'RE NOT THE ONLY ONE

It's not worth it.

And the school team has homophobic students,
playing for them,
because nobody will utter a word about what they'd said.

I'd be done for if they found out I'd grassed on them.
So I won't.

And in my case,
I don't think the coach wouldn't care anyways.

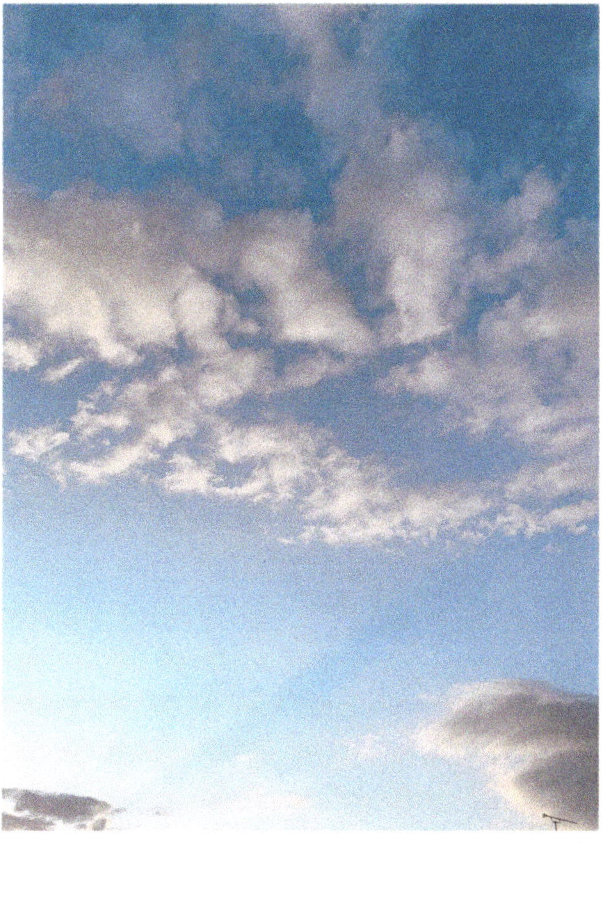

"Leo?" Elijah mumbles, his eyes not leaving his phone.
"Yup." I reply.
"You know you're gay, and I'm trans?"
"Uh-huh, where's this going?" I smirk a little.
"And we've been friends for years?" He pauses for a second,
"And we've never been to Pride together?" Another pause,
"Do you wanna go this year?"
I laugh. It's true,
we've never been to Pride together.
Elijah gets the message that my laugh means 'hell, yes!'.

We met **George** and *Archie* in the hotel lobby, ready to head out on our first day.

"Good sleep?" I ask as way of greeting.
"Well, as good as it could of been with a bed made of chipboard."
"Stop complaining!" George shoved Archie's shoulder.
"It's just honesty, George."
"Right, OK then. Whatever you say." Was the reply, with a joking and somewhat sarcastic shake of the head.
"Alas," I lighten the mood. "Breakfast calls!"

Upon exiting the hotel
and beginning our stroll along the sun-streaked streets,
it is quiet as we take in the architecture around us.

There are wooden crates that line people's balconies
filled to the brim with flowers of great vibrancy,
like an overflowing box of fresh fruits,
ripe and delightful.

There are pools of morning sunlight
where it spills through the gaps in the narrow, dainty lanes.

The front porches and doorsteps of the terraced houses
seem to all have their very own personality,
fastidious in their appearance.

Each terracotta pot is delicately and thoughtfully placed,
as the plants bask and rejoice
 in the warmth of this
Summer's morning.

YOU'RE NOT THE ONLY ONE

The cafe we stop at for breakfast
is tucked away in a streetside nook,
as are many places 'round here.

It seems we're surrounded by a fair few early risers too,
and it is understandable that many may want to get some breakfast outside
before the heat of midday gets too searing.
Like us.

"Woah!" Elijah mumbles as the food arrives,
looking up at the three of us like it's Christmas morning
and he's five years old.

And to be fair, his expression is justified.

My pancakes are stacked high,
dusted with icing sugar and topped with strawberries.
Maple syrup slowly drips from the top pancake, down the stack,
and into a golden pool on the plate below.

Elijah's steaming pastries have an aroma to die for,
butter melts into the cracks of the bread rolls
and small pots of jam and marmalade sit on the side.

Archie and George's apple cake
has sugar on the top of it,
making the tiny crystals glisten in the sunlight.

The espresso is dark,
bittersweet, tangy and soothing
all at once.

YOU'RE NOT THE ONLY ONE

years back

"Would you like to introduce yourself?"
asks the woman opposite me in the circle.
She has large hoop earrings, and is wearing a polka dot jumpsuit.
She leads this discussion group,
and to be honest, as lovely as she is,
I'm scared and I'm nervous,
but I know this is for the best.

"I'm Leo. I'm sixteen."
Everyone is looking at me, but it's not in an intimidating way,
but in a caring and supportive way.
"And I'm gay. I think, no — yeah, I'm gay. That's all."
I paused for a few seconds, gathering my unhealthily dishevelled thoughts.
"I mean. I'm still — I'm still figuring stuff out, you know?"

S
    T
  U
    T
T
  E
      R

"Yeah..."
T
R
A
I
L
I
N
G

O
F
F

S
T
U
T
T
E
R

"Thank you for that Leo," Says the nice lady "It's wonderful to have you here."

Also in the circle there's:

An older man who has been stripped of his confidence after
being victim to a homophobic hate crime at his workplace.

Someone who is coming to terms with their gender identity.

A boy called Archie,
similar age to me,
has brown skin, fingers adorned with silver rings,
looks unbelievably nervous, but I'm pretty sure this

isn't his first time,
like me.
"I'm Archie, and being bisexual and a person of
colour
in my school gets me into trouble with
some of the people in my year
and they
bully me
and I just
don't
understand
why
and I need
to
talk
about it
please.
I hope
that's OK.
I'm rambling,
sorry."

The other boy next to him
("Elijah. I've just transitioned and I feel
more *myself than
ever*.
But, sometimes I still feel
unsure
and
scared
around people.")

YOU'RE NOT THE ONLY ONE

Puts his hand on Archie's thigh
as if to say
it's alright, everything's going to be alright.

And then there's
("George, and I'm not sure where I fit in,
and that's a little intimidating. I mean—I'm not straight,
I know that, but
I don't really—I need to figure things out.")

In this moment, I knew I'd met some
beautiful people.

And we would all get through this
together.

"It's clear to me," Says the lady, "that you are not alone. ***You're not the only one.***"

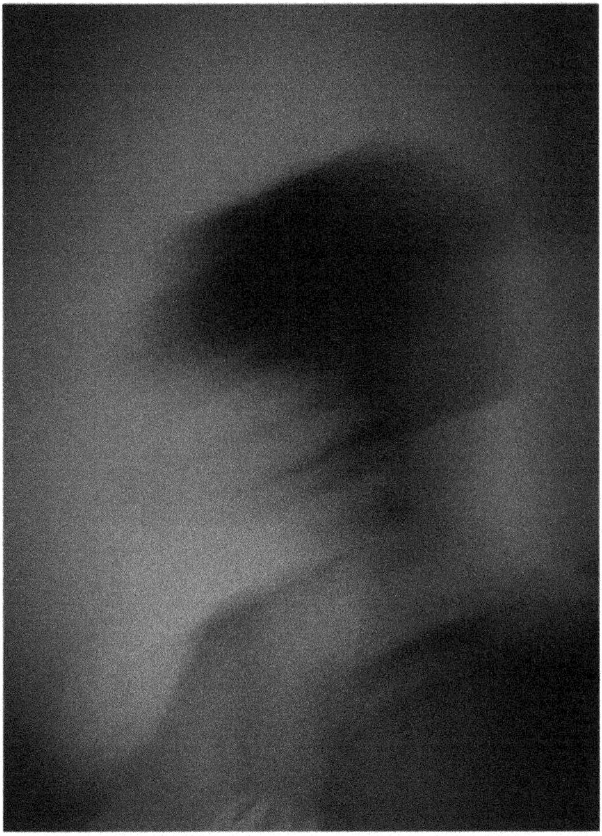

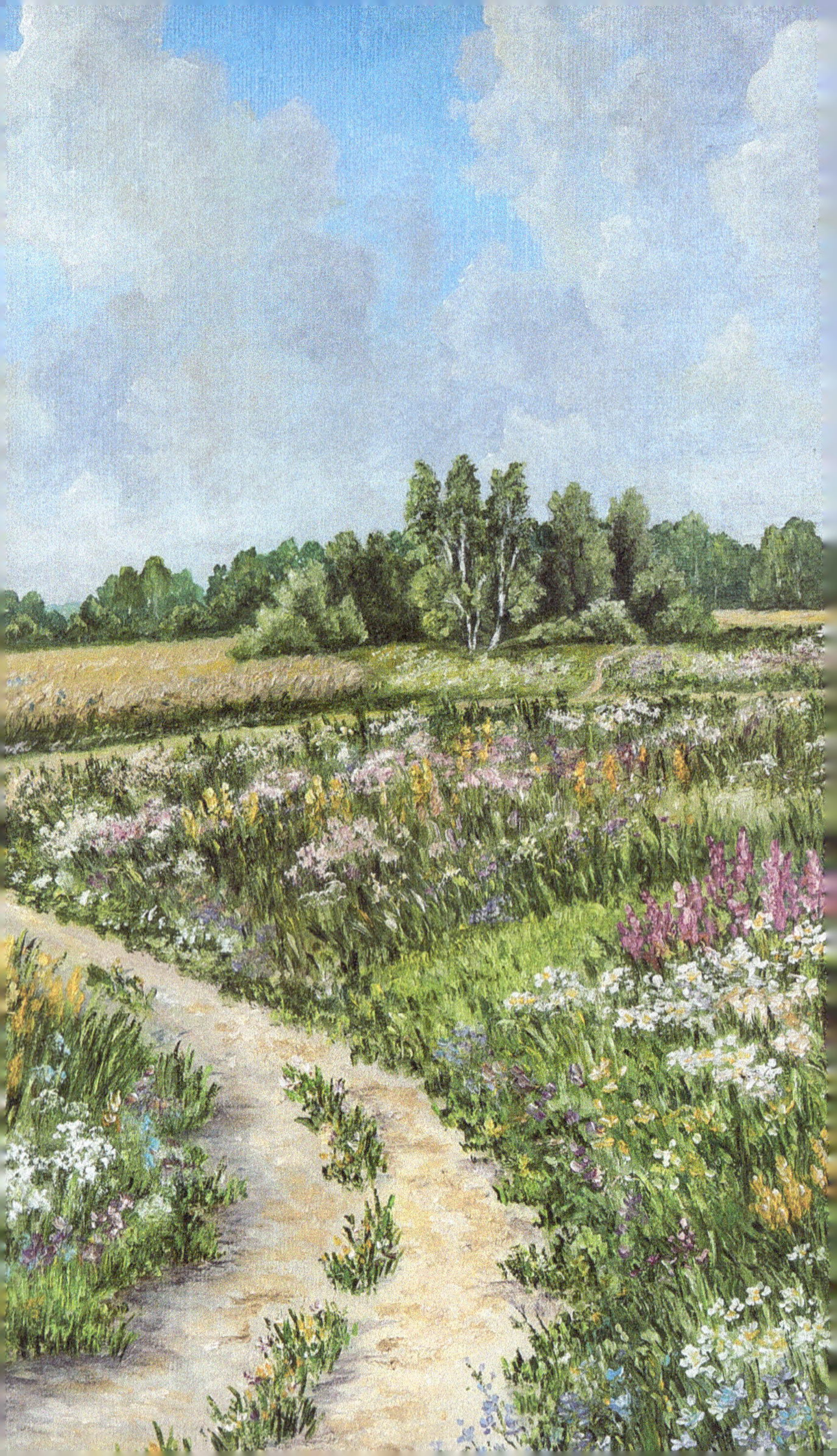

CHAPTER FOUR
DISCOVERY

OLIVER LEWIS

NOTES FROM

YOU'RE NOT THE ONLY ONE

A DISCUSSION GROUP

Labels.
Sometimes confusing.
Often used
to define
you.

YOU'RE NOT THE ONLY ONE

If
the world
wasn't full
of bigots,
we wouldn't need
labels.

Each to
their own.

For some,
they help.

For some,
they don't.

But they always
give a name
to marginalised
groups.

So their

voice

can be

heard

over the

hate.

don't be afraid to
shout

Hate
is a strong word, ## shame we have to use it to describe some people's attitudes and actions against us.

a sign on the wall where our discussion group was held said:

Show **p**assion for the cause,

don't let bullies **r**ack your brains,

fight for the **o**ppressed,

understand and embrace our

diversity.

YOU'RE NOT THE ONLY ONE

...otherwise
progress

                                                                                                   will freeze

If you are
silent
about past trauma
or
bad
experience,
it will grow like a
weed
in the deepest pit of your stomach
and blister.

An ulcer.

YOU'RE NOT THE ONLY ONE

TALK

OLIVER LEWIS

Although the world around
may inflict rage within us,
there's always someone
who can help
snuff the flames.

YOU'RE NOT THE ONLY ONE

Although the world around
may inflict sadness within us,
there's always someone
who can help
dry the eyes.

OLIVER LEWIS

YOU'RE

NOT THE

OLIVER LEWIS

ONLY

YOU'RE NOT THE ONLY ONE

ONE

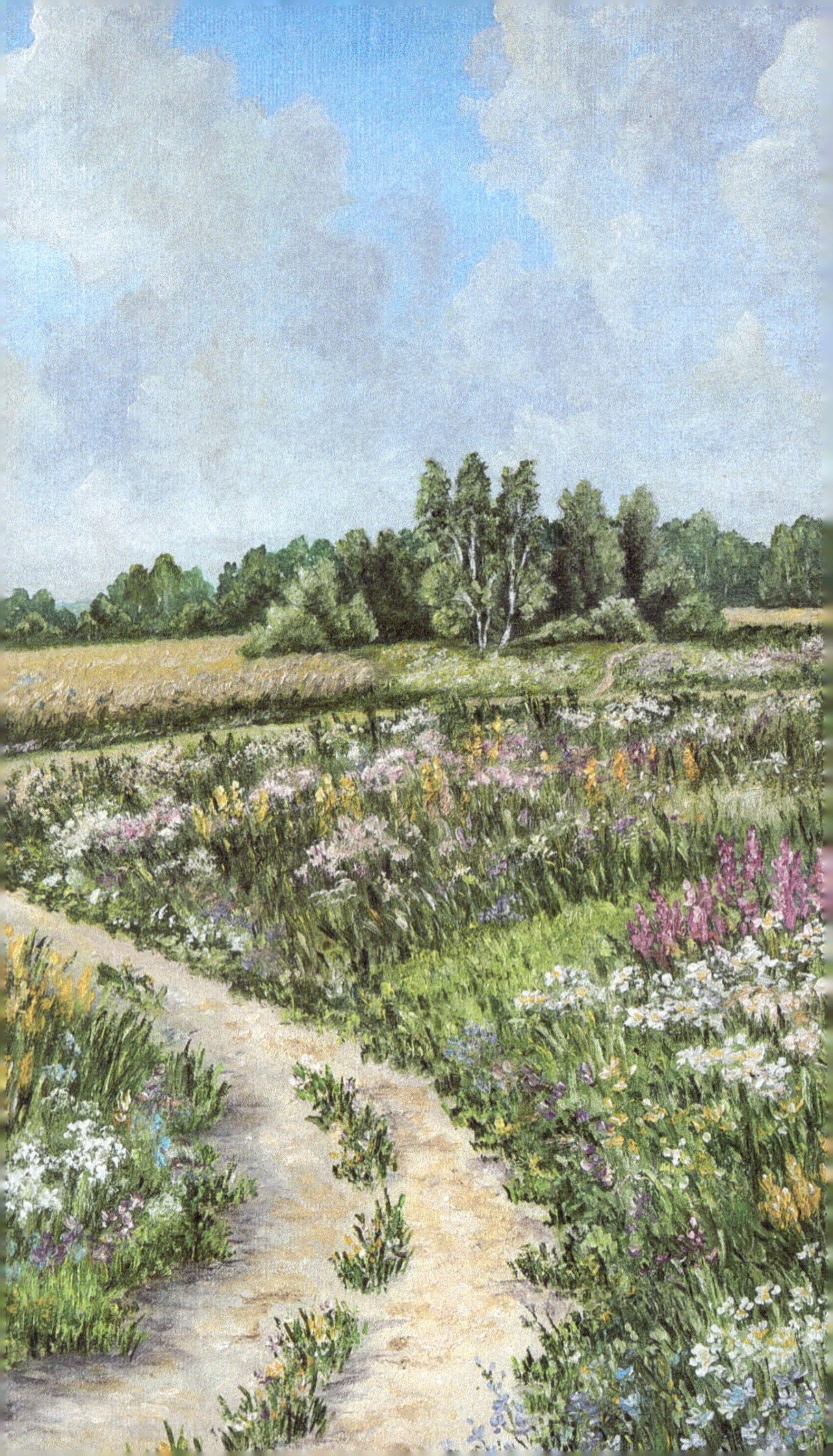

CHAPTER FIVE
FRIENDSHIP

"Do I look good?" George asks.
We're in some thrift shop and he's found these
ridiculously oversized heart-shaped sunglasses.

He's also found a bright green fluffy scarf,
which is now thrown around his shoulders.

"Simply stunning." I say, bluntly.
Elijah seems to be in hysterics,
which is justified.

The old lady who owns the store is glancing over
from her crossword
and giving us disapproving looks.

"You wear 'tis in 'ze store, you mus' buy!"
The old lady says patronisingly.
"You listen to me, eh?"

"Yes, yes," George replies.
"We listen to you!" Adds Archie.

"Well if you're buying it,
you better be wearing it 'round town."
I cut in.

"Sure, why the hell not?!"

YOU'RE NOT THE ONLY ONE

The rest of the day continues in a similar way.

We stop for lunch before
exploring the streets further.

The architecture is still striking,
and exquisite.

Archways curving eloquently,
inviting folk into whatever is on the other side.

Intricate floral and historical carvings
detail the stone, and plaques that lean against pillars.

To think,
these passages have been here
long before me,
long before many vehicles
that can't drive up here.

So rather than being bombarded by the
cacophony of traffic commotion,
we are engulfed by bubbly and cheerful chatter.

We are blanketed by the scent of
bakeries, coffee and musky perfume.

It is remarkable, really.

I've never felt so at home,
peaceful,
contented.

This is truly,
infinitely,
wonderful.

YOU'RE NOT THE ONLY ONE

A few days go by,
and I lose track of time.

Lost in the entrancingly
never-ending days and nights.

Lost in the beauty of this place,
and the people who surround me.

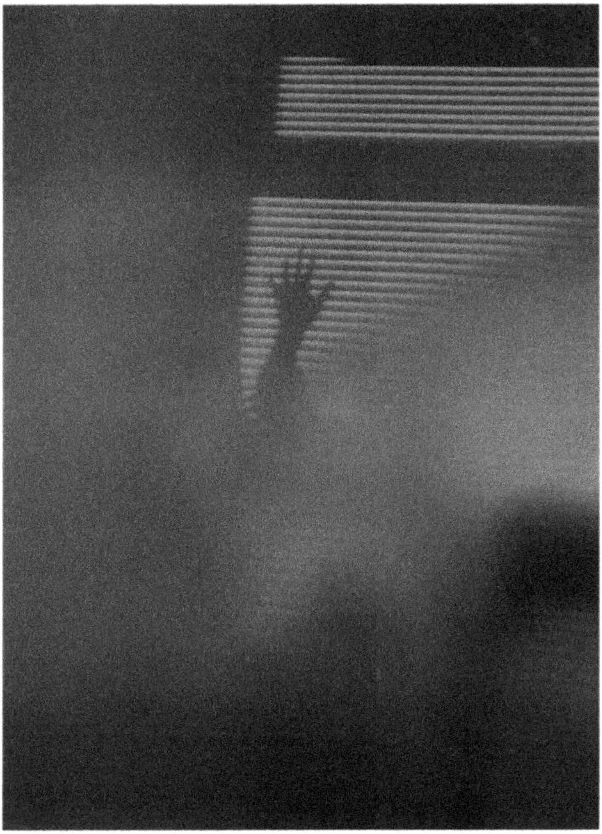

A bumblebee buzzes
under my nose.

Rather than flinch,
or pull away from it,
I watch closely.

The way it simply hovers there for
a few seconds,
before whizzing off to find
a delectable flower.

Allow Mother Nature to breathe,
and thrive.

You'll get along
just fine.

YOU'RE NOT THE ONLY ONE

on that thought

There are no rules
in this life of ours.

Only that
we love.

Yes, we are small
in the grand scheme of things,
but often,
the most minute things
make the biggest difference.

OLIVER LEWIS

Nearing the end of our second week in Italy,
we find a field pretty much in the
middle of nowhere,
and watch the

s

   u

      n

         s

            e

               t.

YOU'RE NOT THE ONLY ONE

When it's almost

pitch black,
we all switch on our phone torches so we can
see each other still.

Amongst general conversation,
Archie, who's been deep in thought asks:
"Why do we have to come out?"
"What'd'ya mean?" Asks Elijah.
"Like, *why*? Who says we *have* to come out?"

We all sit there puzzled.
Because all four of us have already come out,
it's not something that's really
crossed out minds.

"I dunno." Is all I can say.

"Well," Elijah begins

"I don't see why it's a thing either.
I mean, *straight* people don't have to come out,
so I suppose it's just a societal expectation.

The 'norms' in society are clear, because if being who *you are*
doesn't affect you negatively in any way, you fit into societal normality,
else, such as me and George being bisexual, and you being gay, and Elijah being trans,
we have to justify *our*

OLIVER LEWIS

existence
to everyone.

Society has created it's very own mould,
and if you don't fit into it,
you need to let everyone know.

It's so *fucking* sad.

Who even came *up* with that?

It's not like we've never existed!
We've *always* existed."

"That's the thing!" I say now.

And Elijah is right.

It's not like we've never existed!
We've *always* existed.

One day, hopefully,
we'll all be able to fit in seamlessly

YOU'RE NOT THE ONLY ONE

Long into the night
we sing our favourite songs,
and drink cheap beer,
a laugh.

I look up at the sky,
and the stars gaze back at me.
They glisten like diamonds,
like thousands of diamonds shattered across the
deep, never ending blackness of the sky.

The moon stays hidden behind the odd cloud,
occasionally peaking out.

I guess we're all like a moon,
only showing certain aspects of ourselves.

A little at a time,
and when we're with the people we love most
on the clearest of nights,
we are completely ourselves.

Before the cycle starts all over again.

We all put in thirty Euro,
to buy a cheap record player at a vintage store.

The store is filled, stacked floor to ceiling
with an incredibly random assortment of items.

It's a good forty minute walk back to the hotel,
and we toss a coin in a fountain.

The reflection of the small statue at it's centre
ripples and warps in the water below.

"Hey!" George says, waving to himself in the
liquid mirror.

I soak up the history of my surroundings
as we walk.

Lush.

YOU'RE NOT THE ONLY ONE

Back at the hotel, we all go to George and Archie's room.
The new record player is plugged in,
and vinyls are played.

As *Nica Libres At Dusk* plays out,
with it's delicate, floating guitar
sweeping across the room,
we sit and talk.

We talk about September,
about how relieved I am to be away from
some certain people from my now old school.

I realise why I love these friends so dearly.
It's because, with them,
I am simply me,
and they are simply them.

And in this emotional state of
saying why we love each other so much in a somewhat drunken state,
and how proud we are about how far we've all come,
the hours fly by.

Once again, the night is upon us,
but the music plays on.

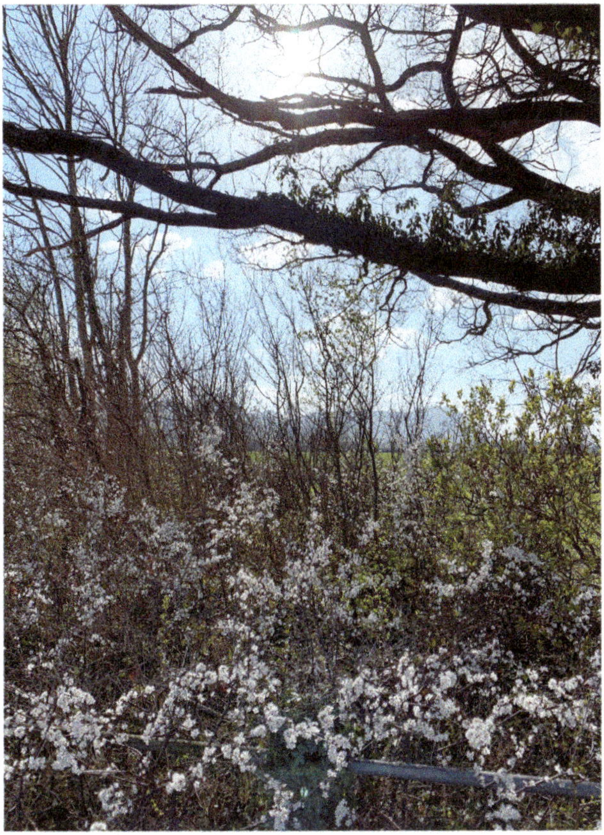

When I wake,
Elijah is reading a battered copy of *The Starless Sea*,
and I ask him:
"How many times have you read that?"

He chuckles quietly, the other two still flat-out.
"Too many times, and yet, I always discover
something new."

"'There is a pirate in the basement...'"
I whisper the opening lines of the book to myself,
which makes Elijah smile.
I love that book too.

I notice the other books splayed across the floor.
There's *The Poppy War* which is mine, of course,
also belonging to me there's *Imaginary Friend,*
and of course there's *Swimming in the Dark*,
which I am making George read, because I just know
he'll love it.

Now a somewhat destroyed copy of *Real Life* is next to
Archie's head,
as it's cover is creased from him shoving it to
vigorously into his backpack.

A pressing of *Hypersonic Missiles* it still sitting
dormant on the turntable,
so ever so quietly,
I sneak over and place the needle on the opening
track.

YOU'RE NOT THE ONLY ONE

It plays softly in the background,
and causes Archie and George to stir.

I take that as my sign with pour a cup of coffee,
because I'm nice like that.

I'm sad that it's our last full day in Italy.
But all the most wonderful things come to an
eventual end.

YOU'RE NOT THE ONLY ONE

We spent that evening at a lake.

You couldn't see the water's edge in the darkness,
so we all walked slowly forward
until we felt the refreshing chill of the cool water at our ankles.

"Three, two, one!" We shouted in unison,
before legging it into the lake.

Water splashed everywhere,
it stung my eyes, but I didn't care.

We all found each other once neck deep,
and just like most nights here in Italy,
laughed and talked
and sang dreadfully.

As ever, the stars were watching over us,
and they twinkled in delight at our joy.

I lay back and let myself float,
and it felt, in that moment,
like I was flying.

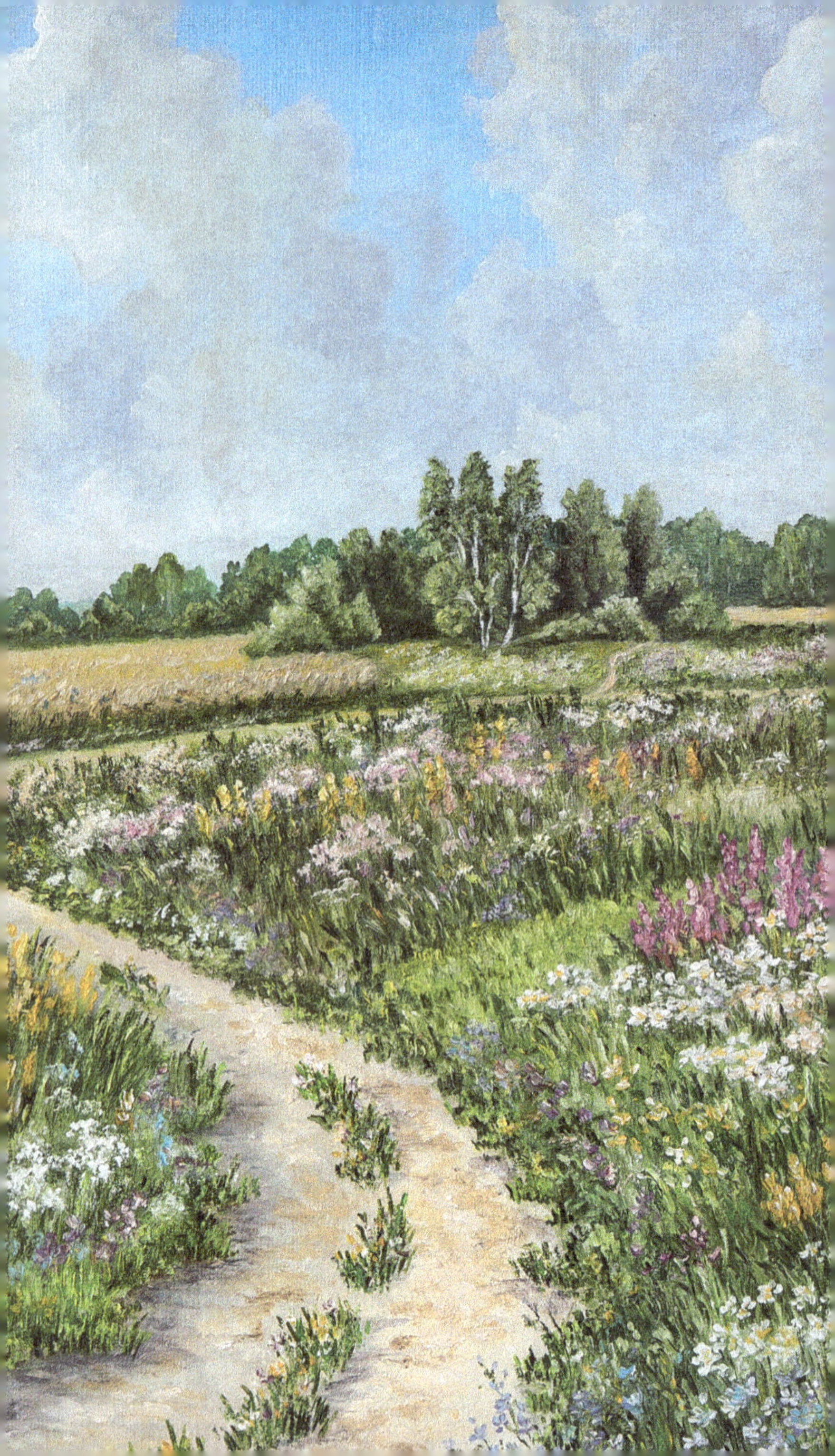

INTERLUDE
FOREST

Figuring things out
for yourself
is difficult,
I know.

But a
storm always
passes by.

YOU'RE NOT THE ONLY ONE

Imagine trekking
through a
forest.

Where the ground
is smooth
and nature

                                                is kind.

OLIVER LEWIS

You can stay
within
this forest
for as long
as you need.

No rush,
take your
time.

YOU'RE NOT THE ONLY ONE

> The smooth ground
> stops you
> from
> tripping
>
> and everything
> is on
> your side.

The
nice
forest.

Ready to leave?
No?

You may stay.

YOU'RE NOT THE ONLY ONE

You build
your dream
home.

Everything you
ever wanted.

You feel
safer
 than ever.

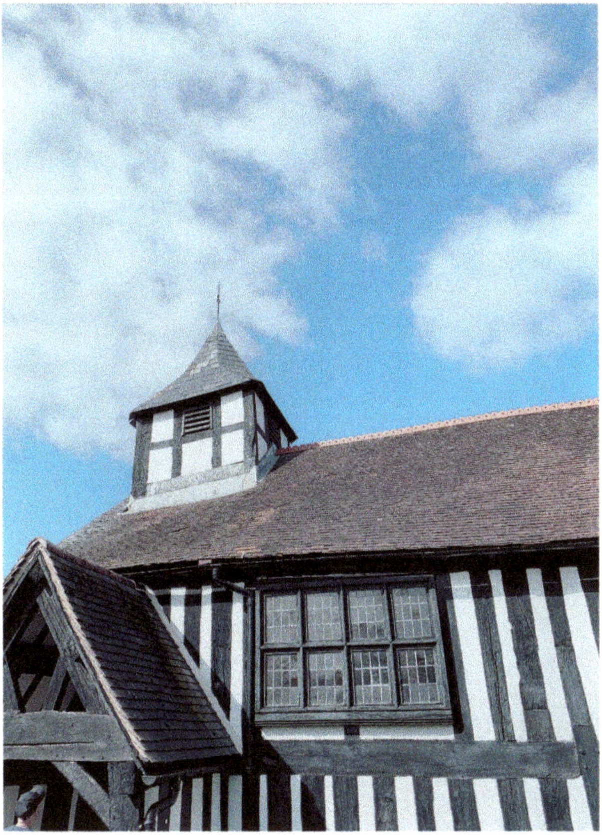

Someone stumbles
to the edge
of your
forest.

Let

them

in

?

YOU'RE NOT THE ONLY ONE

If you do
they'll know
everything.

They could set traps,
you could trip,
or fall.

They probably won't,
but
they
could.

"As long as you don't disturb anything."
You say.
"Simply love me and this forest just how it is."
You say.

YOU'RE NOT THE ONLY ONE

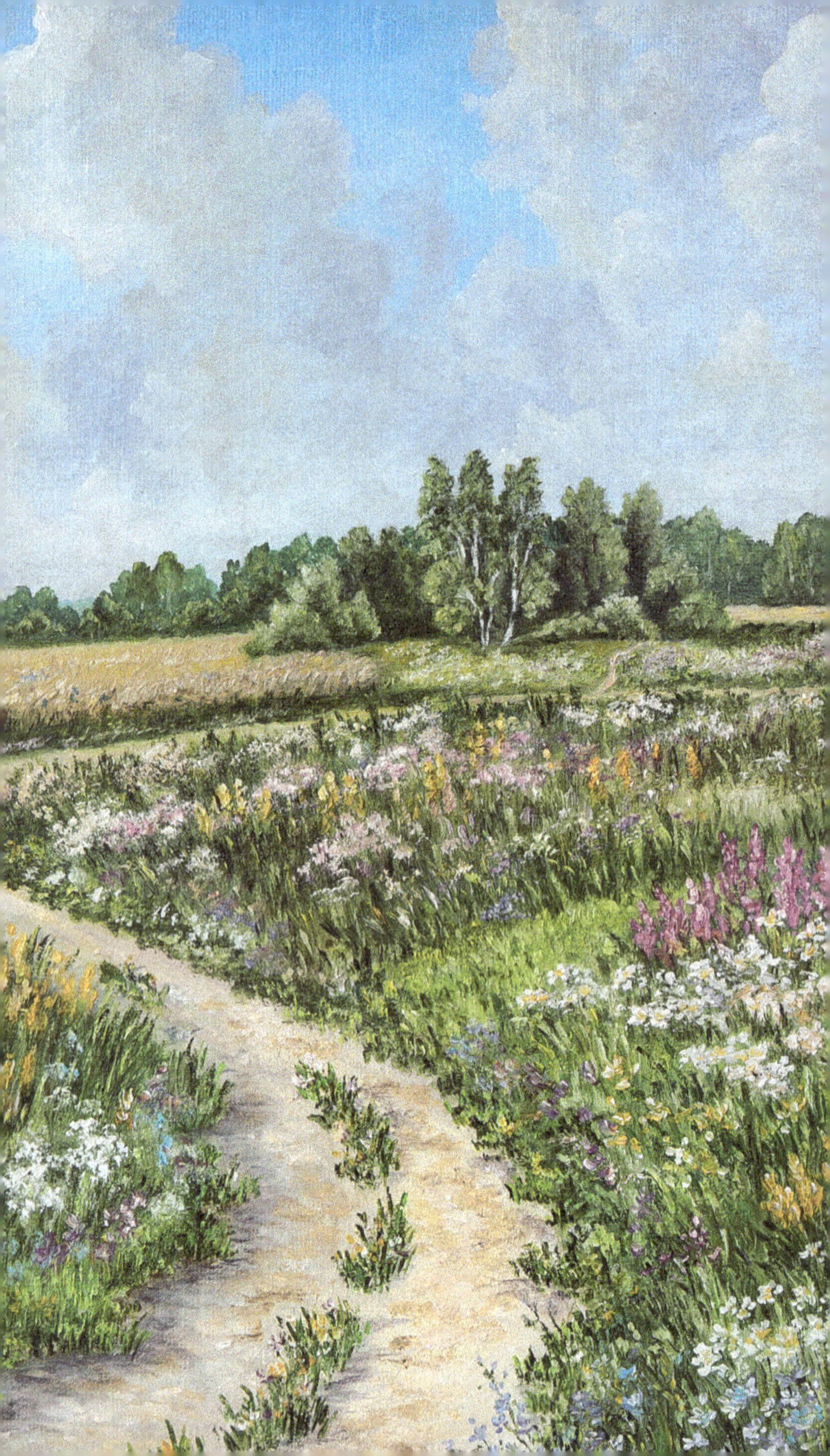

EPILOGUE
PRIDE

After arriving home, I've been quite down,
because after spending so long with just
George, Archie and Elijah,
I feel kind of lonely.

But there's a knock on the door
that I've been waiting for since the minute
I woke up.

I swing the door open,
and Elijah stands on the doorstep looking
incredibly vibrant.

"Wow!" I say.
"Colourful, dude." Matter-of-factly.
"No shit." Elijah chuckles, "Any chance I can come in?"
"God, yeah — sorry."

I have to admit,
It's so brilliant seeing him again.
Even though it's only been
five days.

Soon after, George and Archie arrive,
and we're all ready for Pride.

Although I've been before,
I've never *been* been, as in outfit 'n'everything,
if you get my drift.

YOU'RE NOT THE ONLY ONE

We all have our own huge flags,
and are dressed in a range of bright colours.

It brings me so much joy.

"Shall we head out, then?"

As soon as we hit the city centre,
we see masses of people, that merge into one
huge rainbow.

Our eyes light up.

Streamers hang from balconies,
and people unapologetically blast out
Pet Shop Boys.

The music thrums through my whole being,
I shiver, and get goosebumps.
The hairs on the back of my neck stand on end.

The atmosphere is electric.

There is loud chatter,
people joyfully yelling through megaphones,
whistles being blown,
and *even* a French Bulldog wearing a cloak.

I can't hear myself think
in the best way possible.
Feeling like I've entered another world,
as I go deeper into the celebration.

A parade float edges closer to us,
and people throw confetti from above.

This is one hell of a party.

YOU'RE NOT THE ONLY ONE

The most beautiful and fascinating thing about this is,
every person I see here
has their very own story.

I have mine,
George has his,
Elijah has his,
and Archie has his.

As does the elderly person ahead of me,
as do all the people who brush past me.

Every time I meet the eyes of someone here,
I feel seen,
and I feel warmth,
care,
empathy,
love.

It's magical,
it is simply magical.

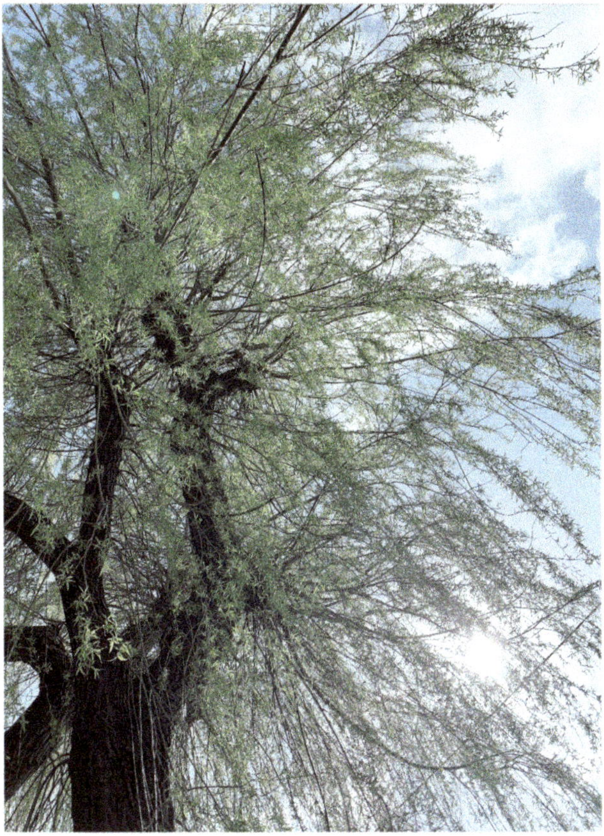

I feel

YOU'RE NOT THE ONLY ONE

understood

I turn my back for one second,
and just like that,
Elijah is gone.

"Where's Elijah ran off to?"
I ask the other two.
"Where *has* he gone?" Archie startles.

We begin working our way
through the crowds,
looking for Elijah.

And as we turn our heads,
we see he's made his way onto a
huge parade float.

George literally cannot stop smiling.
"LEO! LOOK!"
Elijah yells, flailing his arms all over the place.

He's tangled is a load of
streamers and he's now wearing a
sparkly hat someone must have given him.

"COME ON! GUYS, COME ON!"
He beckons us over, and we find our way to some steps
at the back of the float.

Elijah comes pacing over.
"This is so *COOL*!" He shouts into my ear.

Pushing us further into the crowd.

This is the happiest I've ever seen him,
beaming smile, gesturing at everything.
"Welcome aboard!" Someone says from behind us.

So now we're actually a *part* of the parade,
seems we're on a float an'all.

A 2010's *Katy Perry* song blares from an amplifier,
and people wave and scream as we pass.

The four of us clap and sing along to the music,
it's almost like I'm dreaming.

I dance.
And I *never* dance — ever.

But here we are.
I don't know what I look like, nor do I care.

Then we've all got arms round each other,
and we're jumping up and down.

We're yelling the lyrics to pop songs,
and we're on top of the world.

YOU'RE NOT THE ONLY ONE

I've felt quite alone
before now,
It's easier than you think to become isolated
through your own thoughts.

Ever since I've met friends who I can trust,
and left behind people who never cared about me.

I have been let loose.

All there needs to be is
belief.

Belief
that you can be
completely yourself.

In a world without repercussion.

YOU'RE NOT THE ONLY ONE

One day.

In this splendid moment,
time is elastic.

YOU'RE NOT THE ONLY ONE

Can I stay here forever?

"How do you identify, then? If it's alright me asking."
A young man in a white t-shirt and short denim shorts asks me,
he's being genuine and kind.

We've stepped out of the parade, just for a breather, and food.

I smile.
"Well, I always said gay. But the—you know, *nitty-gritty*
has always been a burden. I don't...
I'm not sure I want *that*."
I feel suddenly anxious,
and exposed.

But the man just smiles and says
"Cool!"

"So you don't think that's *weird*?" I ask him.

"Nah! You might just be like asexual or something?"
He throws the term around like it's nothing,
but in reality, it really gets my attention.

"What do you mean?"

"Well—it basically means you are like,
into people but not—
in a ...sexual way."
He says this stuttering, but nonetheless,

nonchalant.

"But I'm — gay?"

"Yeah, you can just be gay asexual."
Again, he says this like it's nothing.

I mean, I've never really thought labels were a great thing, for me, personally.
But for the first time, something feels right, true to me.

Makes sense.
Clicks.

This is a kinda strange conversation for me to have with a random guy.
But it's Pride, who cares?

"So I can be into guys...but just — romantically?"

"Of course!" He reassures me with a smile.
"But you can just keep that to yourself if you like, I don't wanna like overwhelm you or anything.
Just hope I can help."

The other three are there with me the whole time, snacking on a cone of chips.
They look between me and the young man, smiling at my realisation.

I turn the term over in my tongue.
"Gay asexual..." I mumble.
And it feels right.

YOU'RE NOT THE ONLY ONE

I feel like a weight has been lifted off my shoulders.
I feel even better than before.

My eyes well up.
Tears start to slowly roll down my face.

It's the realisation,
it's this celebration,
it's the people,
it's the sense of belonging.

We head back into the parade for
one last time.

Even as it starts going dark,
the streets are alive with colour and light.

As we walk by, a confetti cannon blasts
glitter
into the air.

The sky shimmers,
as it rains down on us
like glimmers of hope.

YOU'RE NOT THE ONLY ONE

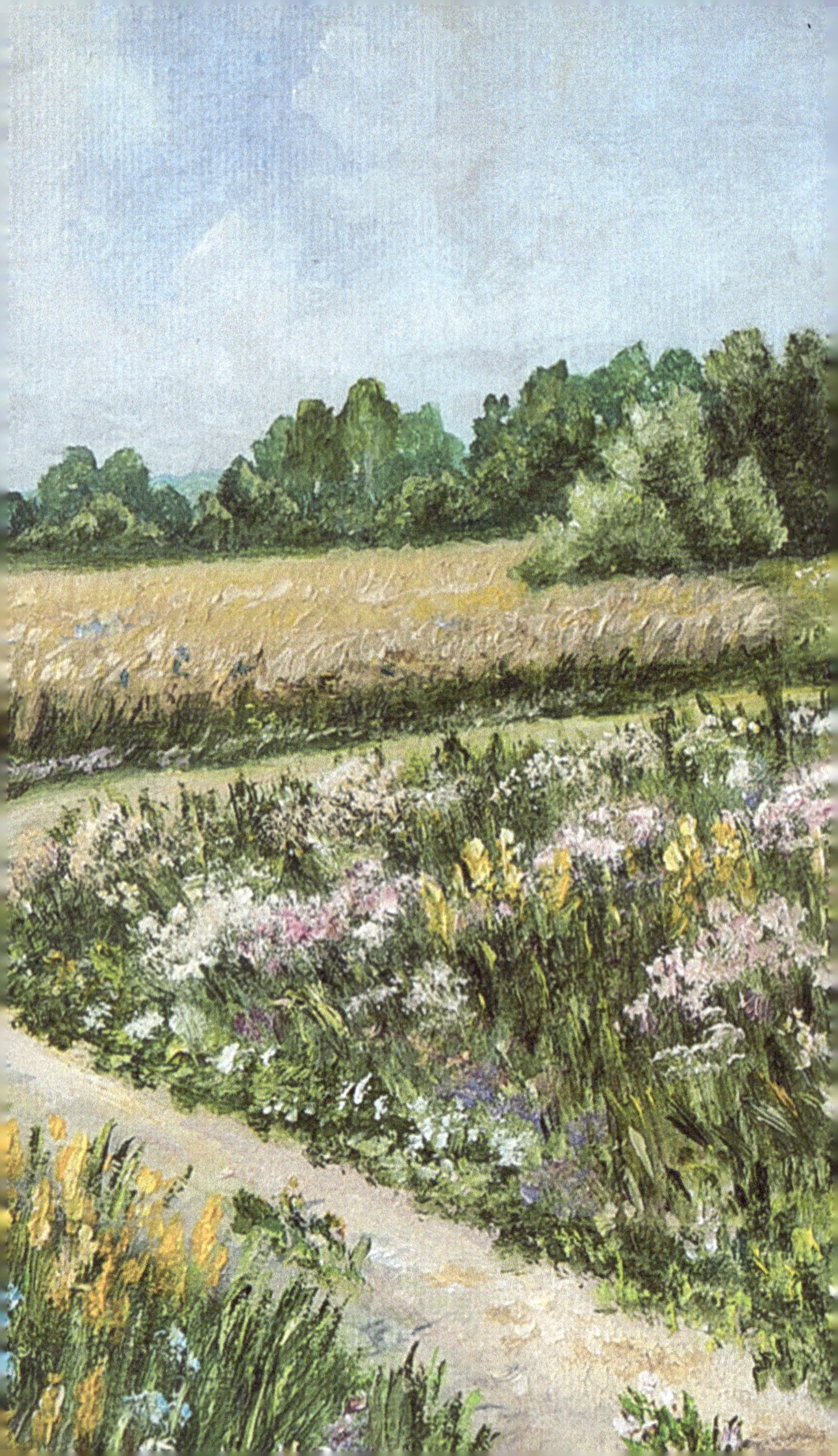

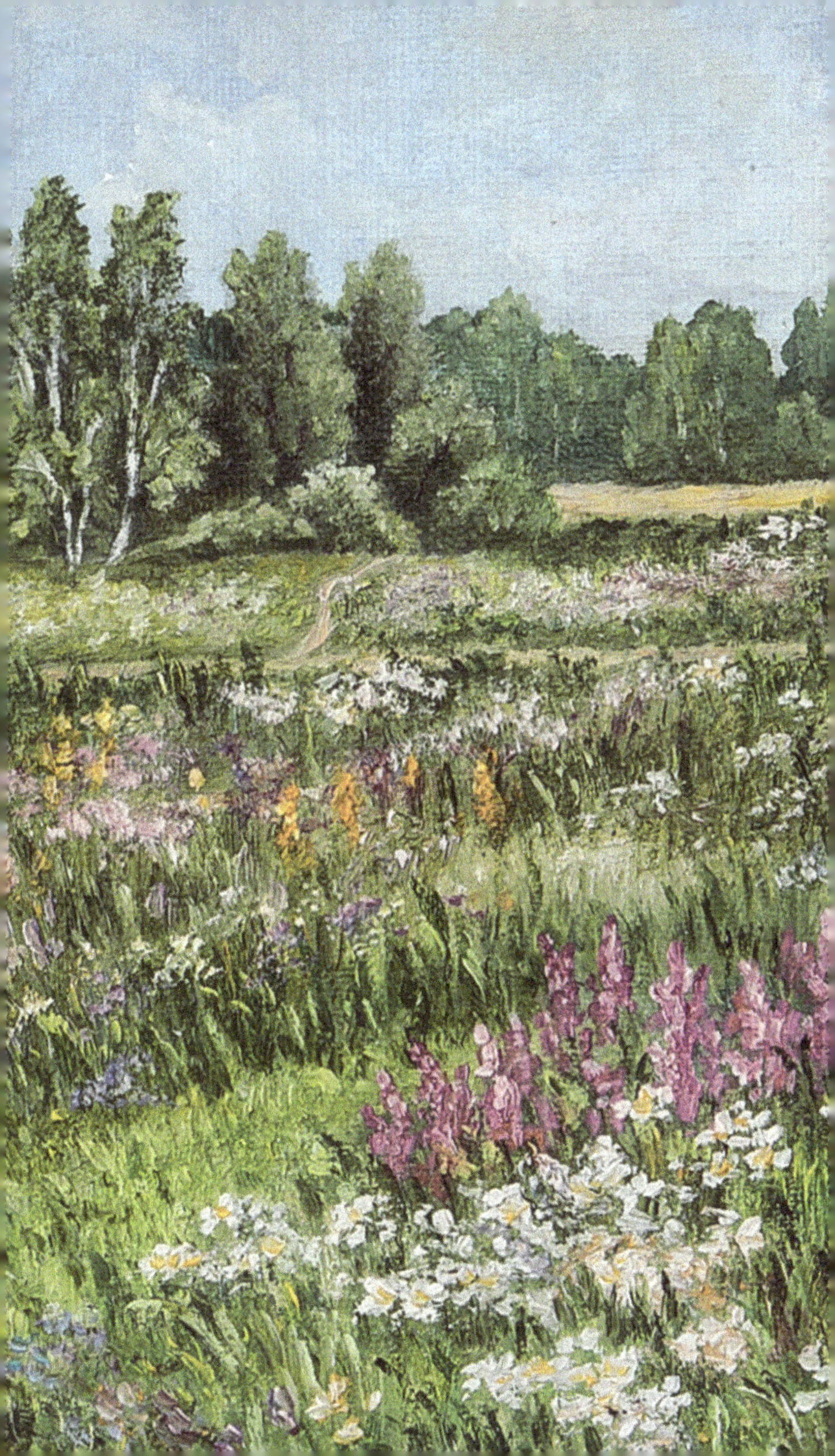

AUTHOR NOTE

It's finally *out* in the world.

I thought I'd leave a little note just here:
*You're Not The Only On*e is a story I have been with for a really long time, and I never knew how to write it, or when to write it, or if I would ever muster up the confidence to release it. But here we are. *Woah*.

I hope you love this story, I hope it reaches the right person. Most of all, I hope it can be appreciated and enjoyed for what it is: not some flowery, lyrical poetry; but an incredibly raw and honest spiel on being a teenager part of the LGBTQ+ community in this day and age, the joys, the lows, the first time you tell someone about it, the times when only you know about it, and the times when you are just starting to figure things out yourself.

I've never written something so close to my own lived experience, which has been, quite frankly, very nerve-racking. There are pieces of me in all these characters, and also pieces of queer stories I've read over the past years by other own voices writers that have inspired me and I look up to, massively.

This writing process has been challenging. I started over two years ago with jottings of thoughts, and things I was observing, reading and so on. About half a year later, I written a skeleton draft titled *Blossom*. And so it begun.

Anyone close to me will tell you how difficult I've found it to let go of this book. I have never re-read and tweaked so obsessively as I have with *You're Not The Only One*, because this was too meaningful a story for me to let go of easy.

This book is for any teenagers who felt the same as any of these characters, if even only a tiny bit. If you see yourself in this story, it is for you. If you simply enjoy this story, it is also, for you.

I hope you love this fictional friendship as much as I have for the past two years, and always.

-Oliver Lewis

ACKNOWLEDGEMENTS

I should start by thanking my parents, my grandparents; you are always first to hold my books in your hands, to read them and fall head first into the stories I have to tell. You have always been there, and I am forever thankful.

My closest friends who make me smile every day, without fail. It is with you that I feel most myself. Here's to more years of laughs and deep chats. I sincerely wish our friendship continues far into the future.

I've never had a teacher so enthusiastic and driven as Mr Biles-Liddell. He is incredibly passionate about English as a subject, and ever since he first knew of my writing journey, has been supportive every step of the way. If you are reading this: your good will, kindness and encouragement is appreciated more than you'll ever believe.

Sam Fender, forever my favourite musician. For creating beautiful music that has gotten me through a lot, has made me smile, and has made me cry; a true storyteller, and a huge inspiration.

Finally, *Nick and Charlie*, two fictional characters created by the sensational Alice Oseman, who have taught me so much about myself.

Thank you so, so much.

MIXTAPE

You're Not The Only One, Sam Fender
Nica Libres At Dusk, Ben Howard
The Great Escape, The Lathums
Falling, The Sherlocks
All We Have Is Now, Royal Blood
Crawling Kingsnake, The Black Keys
Take It Out On Me, White Lies
Make Me Your Queen, Declan McKenna
Claire & Eddie, Kings of Leon
Seventeen Going Under, Sam Fender
Harmony Hall, Vampire Weekend
Lost, Sea Girls
Delicious Things, Wolf Alice
Love Story, Taylor Swift
Hold Out, Sam Fender
It Won't Always Be Like This, Inhaler

RELATED & RECOMMENDED TITLES

Real Life, Brandon Taylor
The Music of What Happens, Bill Konigsberg
Swimming in the Dark, Tomasz Jedrowski
Aristotle and Dante Discover the Secrets of the Universe, Benjamin Alire Saenz
Ziggy Stardust & Me, James Brandon
The House in the Cerulean Sea, TJ Klune
Loveless, Alice Oseman
Shuggie Bain, Douglas Stuart
Felix Ever After, Kacen Callender
Boy Queen, George Lester
Date Me, Bryson Keller, Kevin Van Whye
The Invisible Life of Addie LaRue, V.E. Schwab

TITLES MENTIONED IN THIS BOOK

The Invisible Life of Addie LaRue, V.E. Schwab
Swimming in the Dark, Tomasz Jedrowski
The Starless Sea, Erin Morgenstern
The Poppy War, R.F. Kuang
Imaginary Friend, Stephen Chbosky

FURTHER RESOURCES

ASEXUALITY
Stonewall: https://www.stonewall.org.uk/about-us/news/six-ways-be-ally-asexual-people
AVEN: https://www.asexuality.org/?q=overview.html

BISEXUALITY
bi.org: https://bi.org/en/101

FOR LGBTQ+ SUPPORT
https://lgbt.foundation/

TRANSGENDER
National Centre for Transgender Equality: https://transequality.org/issues/resources/frequently-asked-questions-about-transgender-people

WHY DO WE CELEBRATE PRIDE?
https://www.diversitytrust.org.uk/2020/06/why-do-we-celebrate-gay-pride-month-and-why-does-it-still-matter/

MORE HELP, ADVICE, SUPPORT, INFORMATION AND NEWS:
https://www.stonewall.org.uk/

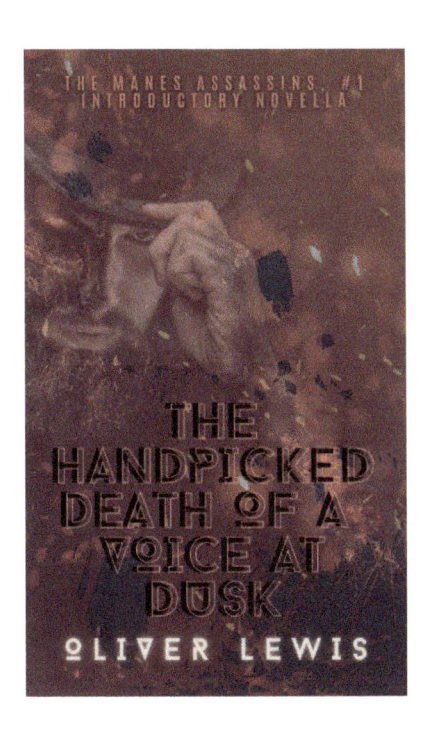

ALSO BY OLIVER LEWIS

In the introductory novella to a three-part story spanning three decades, Oliver Lewis packs a punch with this fast-paced, blood-soaked fantasy.
Zak Vincent, a cold blooded killer who goes by the name of 'The Voice at Dusk', is a top student at the Arkh Ministry. When he makes a drunk deal with his tutor: Master Andrew Harkness to assassinate the Governor, he sparks a civil war between the Ministries. 30 years later, Zak is a captured criminal by the doctor, Sebastian Walter who will punish Zak by death. However, unlike any other criminal, the doctor will allow Zak to choose the way in which he will die.

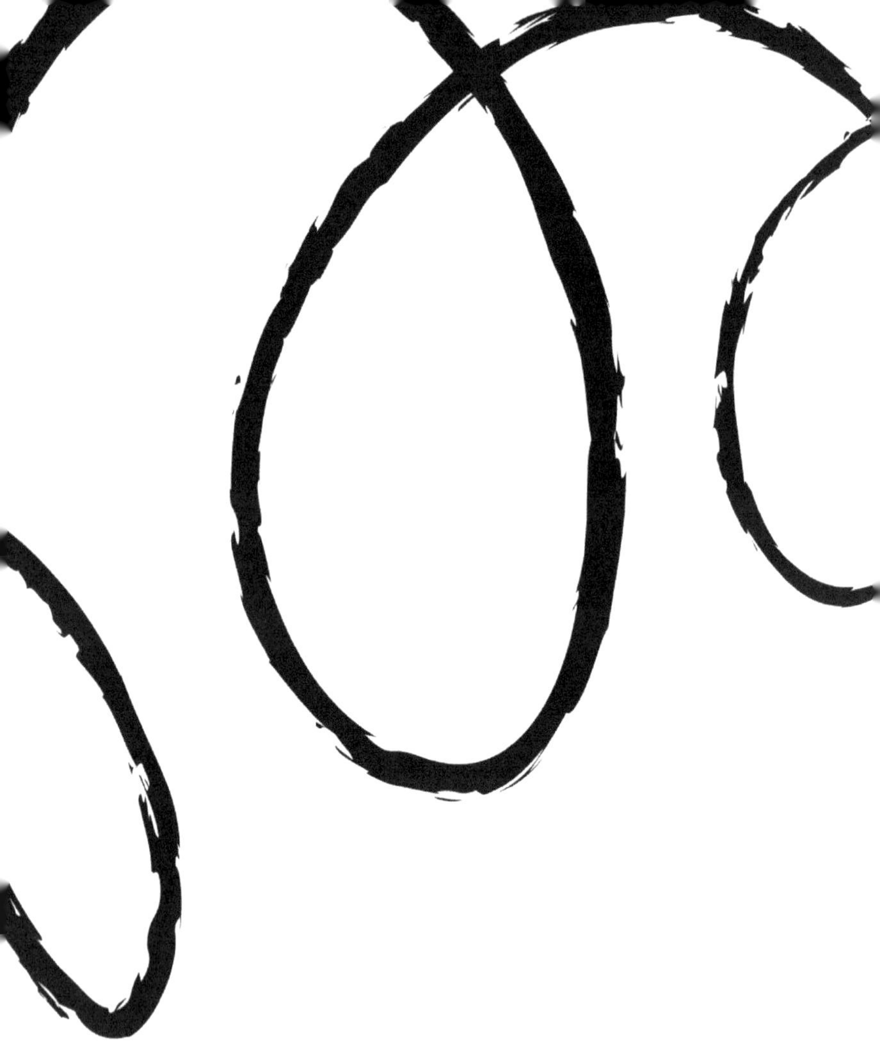

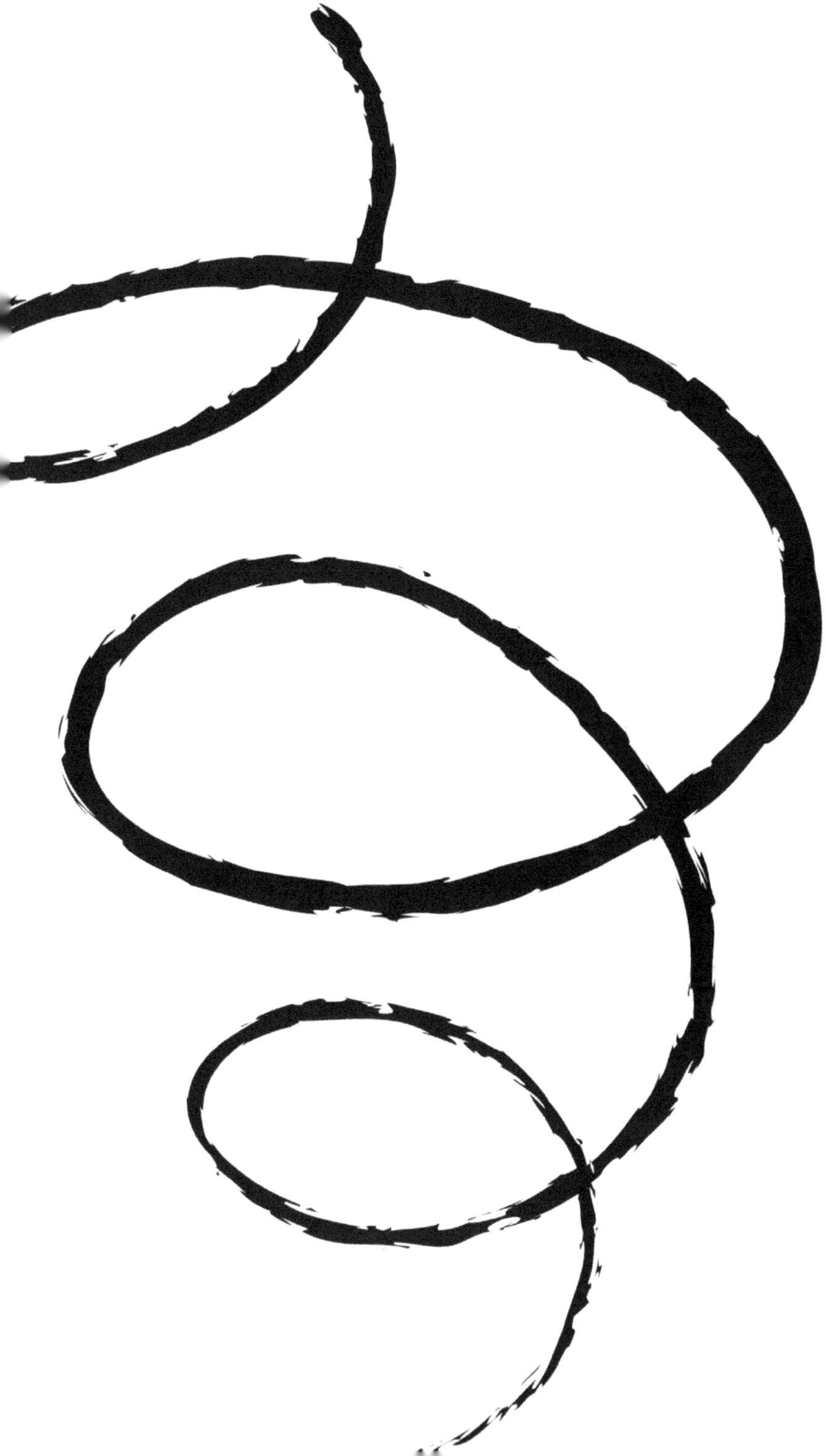

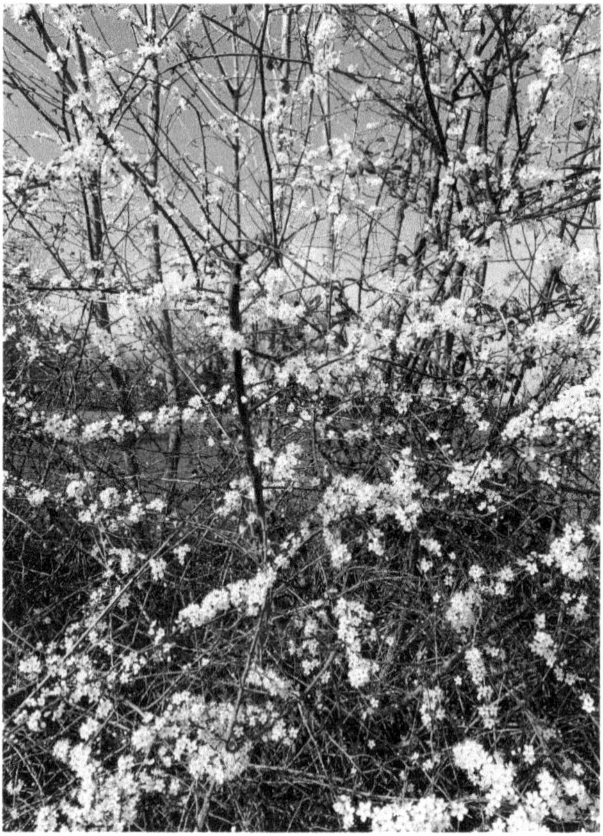

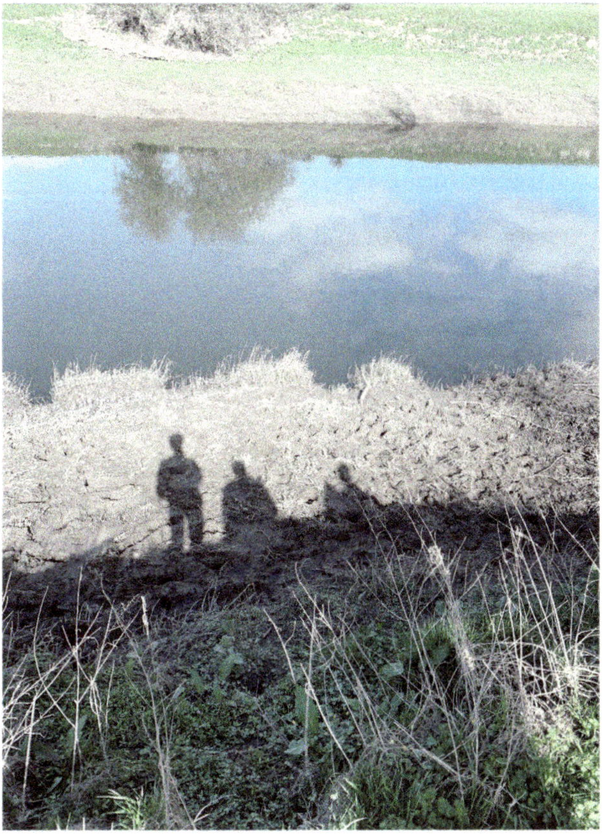

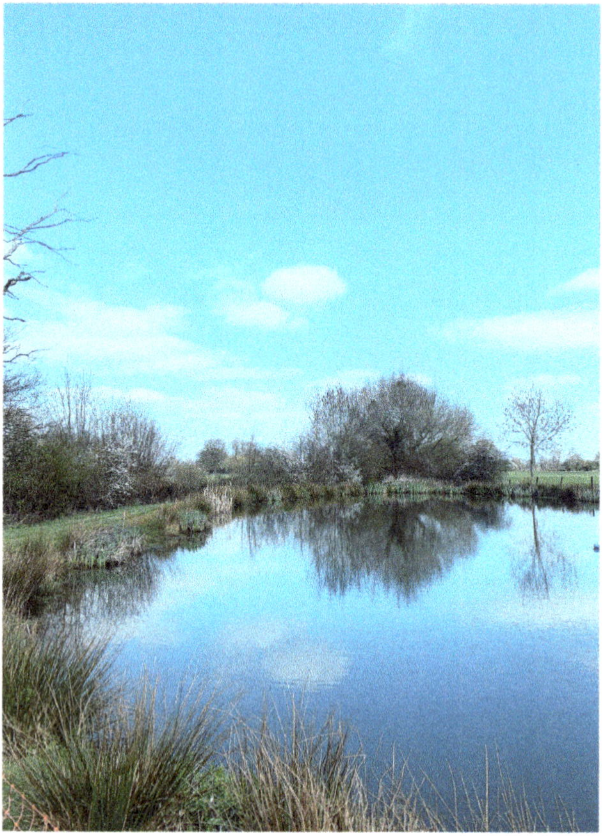

Lightning Source UK Ltd.
Milton Keynes UK
UKHW021531070223
416551UK00005B/564/J

9 781006 624131